Isaac W. Richards

The Refuge

Isaac W. Richards

The Refuge

ISBN/EAN: 9783337335038

Printed in Europe, USA, Canada, Australia, Japan

Cover: Foto ©Andreas Hilbeck / pixelio.de

More available books at **www.hansebooks.com**

"THE REFUGE,"

Drama in Three Acts,

—BY—

I. WOLFF RICHARDS.

"THE REFUGE,"

Drama in Three Acts,

—BY—

I. WOLFF RICHARDS.

CHARACTERS

MAURICIO ALVAREZ, - A SPANISH JEW FLEEING FROM THE INQUISITION.

ROBERTO TALAVERA, - - - - - - - AN ADVENTURER.

BALDOMERO MONTES, - - - - - PIRATE OF THE CARIBBEAN SEA.

DIEGO DELAMAR, - - - CAPTAIN OF THE GALLEON "NUEVO MUNDO."

MIGUEL FRANCIA, - - - - SECRET AGENT OF BALDOMERO MONTES.

RAMON VEGA, - - - - - - OVERSEER OF THE PIRATES' SLAVES.

IGNACIO AMADOR, }
EVARISTO OBREGON, } SLAVES.

CARLOS, JUAN, ALBERTO, ANTONIO, EMILIO PEDRO AND FRANCISCO,—SAILORS, PIRATES, SLAVES. &c.

ESTELA ALVAREZ, - - - - - - - DAUGHTER OF MAURICIO.

ANGELINA MONTES - - - - - - - - WIFE OF BALDOMERO.

DUENDE, - - - - - A CARIB MAIDEN, PET SLAVE OF ANGELINA MONTES.

TIME OF PLAY, END OF THE SIXTEENTH CENTURY.

ACT I.—Scene ; Deck of the Nuevo Mundo at early morning. off the Island of St. Thomas in the Lesser Antilles.

ACT II.—Scene ; Battlements of the Pirates' Castle, with a view of the harbor, on opposite side of which is a hill surmounted by a cross.

ACT III.—Scene ; the Refuge. A Plateau on the mountain side, at the back of which rises a practical eminence surmounted by a cross ; on one side must be shown the harbor and hill with pirates' castle. as if spot were exactly opposite to Scene II.

"THE REFUGE."

ACT I—Scene: Deck of the Nuevo Mundo. Roberto
    Talavera and Miguel Francia discovered.
    Francia at the Helm.

Talavera—You have reckoned well, Francia!

Francia—Be ready, Talavera, to give the signal, when
the ship passes yonder headland.

Talavera—Do you mean the one surmounted by a massive
wooden cross ? Strange symbol that, for a land given over
to the scenes you have described.

Francia—That spot is called "The Refuge." The cross
was planted by some sailors from Columbus' ship when
first the land was visited by Spaniards. Within its shadow,
none of our men, not even the bold Montes, dare venture,
for once a victim of his avarice, escaping from the guard,
fled for safety towards this cliff. He reached the Christian
symbol, and, being nigh spent to death, flung his arms about
it and called to Heaven for help. His enraged pursuers
were upon him, recapture certain, when, of a sudden, a huge
dark cloud shot o'er the clear sky, the thunder rolled among
the hills, the lightning flashed as though it meant to scorch
its way into the very bowels of the earth, which indeed,
must have opened at that instant, for in amazement they
beheld a figure clad in spotless white, with an angelic face,
who, stretching forth her perfect arms, commanded them
away. Seized with a nameless horror, they turned and fled,
and told their comrades of the spirit dwelling by the cross,
who arose from out the earth to save their victim. I needs
must shudder when I think of it.

Talavera—What, men of blood like you overcome by
fancy—bah!

Francia—I'll face any danger that man may offer, but not
that, which belongs to a higher sphere.

Talavera—Had you reflected but a little, the vision may have proved an earthly one. I have not braved what you have, and know not how my courage will serve, but——

Francia—Quick now! hoist the pennant, and run it up and down in quick succession for a dozen times.

Talavera—'Tis scarcely time; we are not near enough.

Francia—We are just right; see yonder battlements reared upon those rocks, just opposite the Refuge?

Talavera—Half hidden by the trailing vines?

Francia—Aye! within those walls our hardy band lies waiting.

Talavera—And their boats?

Francia—Strain well your eyes, and you will see them in the shadow, the cliff throws upon the water. Up with the signal!

> Talavera draws the pennant up and down the masthead quickly.

Talavera—Are we noticed?

Francia—Not yet, may fate ordain, the captain come not upon the deck for a short time. Ah! we are answered, our signal's understood. Now let those on board the Nuevo Mundo pray, if ever they learned how; their doom is sealed.

Talavera—Will you sail directly to the shore?

Francia—Nay; for should we get under lea of those high rocks, the sails will lose their breeze and flap against the mast.

Talavera—And that might rouse the captain earlier than we expected.

Francia—I'll head out to sea again, then tack, and so lose time. Our brave boats will overtake us, and the ship be ours.

> Francia turns tiller and looks at cabin door.

Francia—Hush! here comes my prize.

Talavera (angrily)—The girl?

Francia—The same.

Talavera—Francia, no harm must come to her.

Francia—She is mine

Talavera—Practise cruelty on men who can strike back and I will say nothing, but remember, Francia, the girl is sacred.

Francia—How now, Talavera? Upon the outset, you would pick a quarrel; remember our compact.

Talavera—I have kept it. The rich father and his wealth are in your grasp. Here I stand ready by your side to risk my very life in the obtaining of it if needs be, but I will not see the girl harmed. I swear it by all the good I have rooted from my nature. Remember.

Francia—No more. Here comes the girl.

Enter from cabin Mauricio and Estela Alvarez.

Estela (joyously)—Praise Heaven! we are in sight of land at last.

Alvarez—May this land prove kinder than the one we left and grant a place, poor little wanderer, where we can be at peace. No fearful visions of the Inquisition can pale your gentle face here. What joy is in the sight--a promise of brighter days, a haven for the persecuted.

Estela—So may it prove, dear father; and see! as if to welcome us, boats put from shore and sturdy arms impel them onwards. See now! white sails are hoisted and a merry race begun.

Alvarez—Our hearts bound at this glad sight like those of prisoners who have gained their freedom; no more we'll show a masked countenance to mankind, but live in private as our fathers did at home before the birth of that unhappy edict.

Estela—If only those unhappy ones, who wandered off to drop and die upon their weary road, had fared as we shall fare.

Alvarez—Remember, girl, we are the pioneers of this grand movement. You know I have great wealth, concealed on board this ship, with which to purchase land, before I call from home those families, who, unable to bear with fortitude the great privations of those cast forth from Spain, assumed, as we did, the semblance of another faith.

Estela—The time they longed and prayed for is at hand, from this distance we can see the promise of the soil. See how vegetation carpets all the hills, wafting its luxuriant scent, over the waters, to my enraptured senses.

Alvarez—I'll rouse the Captain to the glorious sight. [Calls at cabin door.] What! Captain! come on deck.

Enter from cabin Captain Diego Delamar.

Capt. D.—The storm has blown over, exhaustion made me sleep longer than I had intended. Why call you, sir?

Alvarez—My faithful Captain, to share our greeting to the New World. See the green hills of promise and the boats that dance upon the waves, sweet messengers of welcome.

Capt. D.—These should be the hills of Hispaniola on our left and Porto Rico on our right.

Goes to side of vessel and looks off, starts as if affrighted.

We are out of our course and have sailed to the East instead of West. This is not the land we should be passing.

Alvarez—Our good captain is by custom rendered indifferent to the scene.

Capt. D. (musing to himself)—Francia and Talavera, the only two on deck. Can they be traitors to me?

Estela Alvarez leans over bulwarks as if observing approach of boats. Mauricio Alvarez regards captain with astonishment.

Alvarez—What moves you, captain?

Capt. D.—Hush! Come on one side, I would say something the lady must not hear.

(They cross to other side of deck.)

Alvarez—Your looks are full of mystery. Does danger threaten us?

Capt. D.—An awful danger, and naught can save us but the utmost coolness and courage.

Alvarez—From what source arises your apprehension?

Capt. D.—Those boats, that seem so welcome in your eyes, are filled with human tigers, followers of the black-hearted Montes of the Virgin group of Islands.

Alvarez—Impossible! I cannot think it.

Capt. D.—Beware your looks, and seem not to be startled, for as I live, Francia and Talavera, who have watched and steered whilst I slept, have purposely put the Nuevo Mundo from out her course.

Alvarez—Then seize, and——

Capt D.—Hush! They are Montes' agents, and I have been duped, as others were before me.

Alvarez—Then summon up the crew and——

Capt. D.—How far the crew is tainted by their treason, I have no means of telling. I must devise a way of taking hold the helm ere they suspect my fearful knowledge.

Alvarez—God of my fathers! my daughter, my sacred trust!

Capt D.—My unhappy master! I have betrayed you by yielding to fatigue.

Alvarez—Have mercy, oh my God! Think of the trouble Thy servant has endured already for the sake of Thy Name and his faith in the creed of his fathers. Turn not the gentle warmth of hope into the chill of despair. Oh, captain! think not of me, but tell me how to save *her*.

Capt. D—Mask your tremor behind a bold front, and when I have gained possession of the helm I'll do my best to distance them.

Alvarez—Together we can suddenly overpower those at the helm; let me assist, ere they suspect ——

Capt. D.—Not so, alone I'll boldly order them below. If none among the crew are won over to their side they dare not disobey me, if otherwise——

Alvarez—What then?

Capt. D.—I fear our fate is sealed; still, should they disobey my orders, I'll dagger them ere they know my purpose Now go quietly towards your daughter.

Mauricio Alvarez joins his daughter. Captain Delamar approaches the two at the helm.

Capt. D.—Go below and send up Carlos to the helm. You are both overworked and need rest.

Francia—I feel fresh, sir, and can still remain at my post, you are more in need of it, I pray you sleep again.

Capt. D.—Go on the instant, both of you, your eyelids droop so that you see not the vessel's course, leave me the helm and send up Carlos. Go both! I command it!

> Feels under his doublet with one hand and grasps tiller with other.

> Francia and Talavera yield and exit at forward hatch.

Alvarez—Child, Heaven's wrath pursues us even here, we have fled from danger, but to meet with greater.

Estela—Alas! what threatens now?

Alvarez—Beam not from your eyes, soft glances of welcome on · yon boats, for should they reach our ship, a fate awaits us worse than death.

Estela—What fate can be harder than the one we have left behind?

Alvarez—Had we faced that' our bodies may, indeed, have suffered torture, which our minds, firm in their belief, would have borne us up against.

Estela—Not alone the torture would we have faced, but the mocking crowd deriding our misery and scoffing our noblest thoughts.

Alvarez—At least they, who there inflicted suffering, did so in religion's name, and were men of conscience were they ever so cruel.

Estela—Conscience, aye! inasmuch that when they saw our wills unalterable, they mercifully gave us death.

Alvarez—Aye! but they, who every moment gain upon us, are men lost to the very name of humanity. No beast that haunts the wildest jungle can compare with man's ferocity, when once the fire of conscience is wholly quenched within him, and for your honor, dearer to me than your life, I tremble.

Estela—But why despair? Have we not brave men on board, and arms? Speak to the captain; bid him rouse the crew.

Capt. D.—Our greater safety lies in speed. They, who pursue, outnumber us a score to one. If overtaken, we are doomed.

Alvarez—At least we are men and can sell our lives dearly. The wretches will not hesitate to slay us, but if they lay hands upon my jewel, pure and unstained, radiant in her beauty, what will become of her?

Estela—Let the weak resort to cunning, and since danger doubles for my sex, let me assume man's garb and pass for your son.

Alvarez—This is against our Holy Law.

Estela—But we have not in these days, as of old, wise men who can commune with God and teach His bidding. The wisest of us can but think with earthly power; above this earth, we none of us can soar.

Alvarez—You are as wise as you are pure, and faithful to God's law, and I am sure, your honor being at stake, the means proposed will be acceptable. But where to find the dress?

Estela—I have it in my chest.

Alvarez—What! A suit of man's clothing?

Estela—A memory of that poor martyred one of your own father's family, dragged behind the frowning walls of the Inquisition, despite his youth.

Alvarez—And whose history and bright example have been as a rock of strength, for any of our family when faced with danger.

Estela—Oft have I wet the graceful garments with my tears, when none were near to see me.

Alvarez—Perhaps 'twas God's own provision, for the part you have to play.

Estela—I'll quickly put it on.

Alvarez--Quick ! Quick ! Clip short your raven locks and join me, that if we die we enter Heaven's gates together.

[Estela exits into cabin.]

Capt. D.—As long as these good boards remain together, your treasure is well hidden, be our pursuers as sharp as wolves or cunning as foxes, I warrant they can never bring that to light.

Alvarez—But their habit is to fire any ship that comes in their possession.

Capt. D.—The Nuevo Mundo will be a boon to them, and though their hideous flag will float, where now waves the proud ensign of Spain, as long as they leave the ship intact, let your hope live to recover it some day.

Alvarez—Do they gain upon us ?

Capt. D.—Aye, their light craft scud through the waters like hounds upon the forest game.

Alvarez--We must be bold enough to fight.

Capt. D.—'Tis the only chance that's left, pray play the boatswain part awhile, and summon up the crew, name by name, as I shall call them out.

Alvarez—Consider for the time, that I am as one beneath you, and order as you seem fit.

[Goes to forward hacth.]

Capt. D. Call Carlos, the villains have not sent him.

Alvarez—(Calling down hatch). Carlos !

[Carlos comes on deck.]

Capt. D.—Call Juan !

Alvarez—(As before). Juan !

[Juan comes on deck.]

Capt. D.—Call Alberto !

Alvarez—Alberto !

[Alberto comes on deck.]

Capt. D.—Antonio !

Alvarez—Antonio !

[Antonio comes on deck].

Capt. D.—Emelio, Pedro, Francisco, Enrique.
Alvarez—Emilio, Pedro, Francisco, Enrique.

[They come on deck.]

Capt. D.—Men, have you the hearts of Spaniards ? Love you our country's flag. Dare you defend its honor ?

[Sailors cheer "aye" in unison.]

Capt. D.—Look athwart our quarter at yonder craft, your trained eyes can tell their nature at a glance.
Carlos—Holy Madonna ! We are undone.
Juan—To arms !
Capt. D.—Ha brave fellows ! We shall welcome them with blows that stagger.
Carlos—Command us, Captain !
Juan—We will resist unto the death !
Capt. D.—Carlos, to the helm ! Keep the ship headed for yonder point of land, Juan and Alberto, haul out the cannon on either port, the rest seize on spikes and stand ready to repel the villains.

[They obey the captain's orders, hauling out the cannon and arming themselves with spikes, kept in a rack around the mast.]

Capt. D.—(To Mauricio Alvarez). Remain upon the deck and urge the men, I'll below, and with the help of those we have not summoned, place both those villains in irons.
Alvarez—That done, return with the others to aid in the defence.

[Captain exits at forehatch.]

Alvarez—(To the men). Spain, thou art the mother of the valiant ; in each brave eye I see a stern resolve, in each set face, there is reflected the dazzling glow of patriotism to our flag and to humanity. The worst that can befall such men is the end that heroes hope for ; stand firm, brave fellows, and we are delivered.

> Enter from cabin, Estela Alvarez dressed as a
> boy, armed with a cutlass.

Estela—My father, behold thy son!

Alvarez—Ha! Cans't thou assume so well, but what meanest thou by this vile weapon? Your slight hand shall not be bruised by its rough hilt; give that to me.

Estela—Nay, shall I reserve no defense?

Alvarez—My God! You have, it seems, the courage of a man. What means that lurking mischief in your eye bright as the Orient? Speak! What would you with this weapon?

Estela—To slay no man, nor yet unsex myself, but think you, my father, I can forget your blood is in my veins, and when 'tis necessary to choose between that dread alternative of dishonor and death, should my disguise fail to screen me, think you, I'll hesitate?

Alvarez—Oh, Spain! Spain! Couldst thou but know the spirit of those cast forth from thy bosom! My noble child, my sweet Estela, give me that weapon.

> [Takes cutlass from her.]

Estela (aside)—Within my bosom I have concealed a smaller weapon.

Alvarez—Should it please Heaven that *you* escape this trying hour unscathed, remember girl, the treasure I have guarded as my life, that which I hold in trust for the persecuted ones in Spain, lies concealed beneath the boarding of the hold, just where the foremast is stepped in the keel.

Estela—I will remember.

Alvarez—My private wealth, much smaller than the other, but valuable for thy sake, to make assured your future welfare, is boarded up behind the wainscot of my berth in the cabin.

> [Captain's voice heard below.]

Capt. D.—Help! Ah, I perish!

Alvarez—What means that cry? Treachery below. To his aid men.

> Men with spikes rush to forward hatch, from which enter Francia with bloody dagger, followed closely by Talavera.

Alvarez—Seize upon those two. I'll hasten to the captain.

[Exits down hatch.]

Carlos—Man the bulwarks, men, they are near at hand.

> Sailors mount on bulwarks, raising their spikes.

Talavera (to Francia)—Inhuman coward, to strike down a brave man in that way.

Francia—Fool! Have you lost your wits? 'Tis rather late now for such moralizing, our boats are on us. If at this moment you weaken and turn false, your life shall answer for it. (Looking around.) Where has that pretty little bird concealed herself?

Talavera—Francia, take care. Think of the solemn oath I've taken as regards the girl.

Francia—A plague on all your oaths, I care nothing for them. I'll search out my prize in the face of all your threats.

> Looks around and walks along deck, followed as before by Talavera. Clash of arms and rattling of chains heard, mingled with men's shouts, as if pirates were climbing up sides of vessel. Francia springs on bulwarks.

Francia—Ha! brave comrades, they are here. We have gained our cause.

Estela (before door of cabin)—Father! Father! Stand by me, they are upon us.

Francia (leaping from bulwarks)—Ha! I have found you out, my little captive, eh!

> Runs towards her, followed stealthily by Talavera.

Think you to fool me? I see through that disguise, poor, silly thing. You are mine, and thus I take you.

> Lays hold of her, forcing her on her knees. Talavera throws his arms around Francia, from behind.

Talavera—And thus I keep my oath!

> Forces Francia over the rail into the sea, as Mauricio Alvarez rushes from forward hatch.

Alvarez—Our noble Captain is slain.

Talavera—Aye! and you are my prisoner; but fear not, say nothing, for I swear by all the holy saints to save you and your daughter.

CURTAIN.

ACT II.—SCENE: BATTLEMENTS OF MONTES' CASTLE.
IGNACIO AMADOR AND EVARISTO OBREGON DIS-
COVERED CLEANING UP THE RAMPARTS.

Obregon—Amador, since it is the will of that accursed
Vega that we be served short rations for our display of ill
temper, I'll teach you a serviceable trick under the circum-
stances.

Amador—I know what you are about to say, Obregon.

Obregon—What, my keen witted slave?

Amador—You would tell me to fill the gap in my stomach
with fresh air, and thus stop the gnawing; an old joke, in
faith, and I am in no humor for joking.

Obregon—You wrong me, fresh air makes only a cold breakfast. I would bid you do as I am doing, tie your waist
strings closer about you, and stop the air from getting in
and then your stomach will feel warmer and more com-
forted.

Amador—What a man you are, to let even your misery
serve as food for jest.

Obregon—Our good time will come Amador, fear not; and
if we pine away now, we cannot live to enjoy it, therefore
laugh present sorrow away.

Amador—I can't, my stomach is too empty; accursed
villians! What have they done with that handsome boy
they captured lately?

Obregon—The lady Montes keeps him in her service.

Amador—Ah! the lady Montes, that one bright light,
amid the darkened souls of this infernal den.

Obregon—Did you notice, Amador, the new lieutenant of
the pirate, who came on board the Nuevo Mundo?

Amador—Aye! I take good notice of each one of the
infernal crew, so that if fortune change for us some day, I
can bear true witness against them, and enjoy their hang-
ing.

Obregon—Nay, this same fellow has some secret purpose
locked within him, he gazed at me on passing, and looked
so earnestly, as if cogitating in this wise to himself—"I

wonder if this slave would have the courage to strike a blow for freedom." Know you, that hope has sprung up in my breast since his arrival?

Amador—Sh! Speak lower, remember the length of that accursed Vega's ears, if you have reason for the hope, and any of the villians overheard you ——

> A loaf of bread is hurled from an abutment in the battlements, and strikes Amador in the back.

Amador—(Straightening up in alarm ;) Oh! I am slain.

Obregon—Nay, this is not a death dealing instrument, but life giving bread. (Picks it up)

Amador (eagerly)—Br—br—bread! Did you say bread? Halves, if you love me, Obregon!

Obregon (looking around in wonder)—Does Heaven drop food to the starved from the skies? Wherever did it come from?

Amador—Nay, our wits will be in better condition for the solving of that mystery when we have fortified our stomachs. Fall to, Obregon, fall to, and appease your craving.

> Obregon breaks loaf in two and gives half to Amador. They cram their mouths full, eating ravenously for a few seconds.

Obregon (suddenly coughing and sputtering. Amador pounds him on back)—Hola! what's here?

> [Draws paper out of his mouth.]

Amador—A paper, as I hope for mercy, and just like the wraps we have for drugs and medicines in Spain.

Obregon—'Twas embedded in the bread.

Amador—This is some trick of that cold-hearted wretch Ramon.

Obregon—What mean you, Amador?

> [Examines paper.]

Amador—That wrap contained some drug with which the bread is poisoned. He would kill a slave for the sport of witnessing his torture.

Obregon—Bah! You are nervous.

Amador—He will be here presently to laugh at our agony. Be not incredulous. I have sharp pains within—I thought it due to the sudden overloading of my stomach, but it's clear to me now.

> Passes his hands up and down, ruefully over his stomach.

Obregon—This paper has writing on it. Have you forgotten how to read.

Amador—That I have not. Give me the paper.

> Obregon passes it to him. He reads:
> "I am not what I seem, but may accomplish your freedom if you are willing to aid me. If willing, when you see me cross my fingers to you in passing, make the same signal in return "

Obregon—What is the signature to the paper ?

Amador—No signature at all.

Obregon—It matters not ; my life on it, it is the writing of the new lieutenant. He has thrown us this bread with more purposes than one. Eat, Amador, and gain strength.

Amador—I eat thankfully in faith.

Obregon—Ha! ha! Tear that note up in tiny bits, and throw it to the wind.

Amador—Aye! aye ! presently, when we descend to the yard, so no fragments can be found.

Obregon—Ha! ha! You are not half so downcast as you were a moment since.

Amador—Ha! ha!

Obregon—No sharp pains, within, eh? Ha! ha!

Amador—No! eh! yes! That is; they have left me as suddenly as they came.

Obregon—The bread was only poisoned with a little hope, that's all. Nothing more is to be done here. Take up your water-pail, and let us descend to the yard.

[Rests his water-pail on bulwarks]

> Talavera enters from behind abutment and crosses his fingers to them. They return the signal. Talavera exits in castle.

Obreyon—'Tis as I thought, Amador.

Amador—Heaven be praised for it, Obregon. There is that wretch, Ramon, leaning against the wall below us.

[Points over bulwarks.]

Obregon—I have a measure or two of water left in my pail. Shall I shower it on him.

Amador—Art mad? Have you no sense? 'Twill be the death of us.

Obreyon—Nay, he sees us not, and 'tis only a very mild revenge for our fast.

[Empties pail over bulwark. Shouts from below.]

Amador—Fly for your life, he is bounding up the steps like a tiger. This way.

> They run off. Enter Baldomero Montes and Roberto Talavera from castle, Ramon Vega from centre.

Montes—Vega, remain within call, I shall need you in a moment.

Vega—Saw you any slaves here?

Montes—None. Have any fled?

Vega—They hurled their filthy water within an inch of me. I will be in the castle.

[Exits in castle.]

Montes—I have been duped by that accursed Francia, and would this hand had been the means of hurling him to death.

Talavera—What word was it he sent you out from Spain?

Montes—He promised this should be the richest prize I had ever taken, and save the Neuvo Mundo, which in itself is worth the killing of a dozen men, I have nothing but a few miserable slaves. By the saints! I have never seen men fight so valiantly to save so little.

Talavera—I am no less a dupe than you are.

Montes—How fell you in with Francia?

Talavera—It was in Cadiz. As you can fancy, my life has not led strictly in the paths of honor. I had just been thrown upon the world from out of prison.

Montes—Without the means of living, I suppose?

Talavera—I knew not where to look for food or shelter, and wandering to the shipping I met Francia.

Montes—And he broached the enterprise at once?

Talavera—No; he gave me money for my wants, and plying me with wine, won me to his side.

Montes—And in what way were you to aid his scheme?

Talavera—Disguised as an officer of the Inquisition, I was to present myself at the house of Alvarez, the Jew, who lived, ostensibly, a Catholic.

Montes—And urge him to this journey?

Talavera—Aye, by swearing that he had been betrayed, and that the Inquisitors were on his track. He at once embarked upon the Nuevo Mundo, and Francia, who had shipped as mate, secured for me a berth on board.

Montes—The rest you left to fortune?

Talavera—We did, and fortune seemed to favor us. A storm arose, the crew worked so that they fell from sheer exhaustion, the Captain as soon as danger ceased slept soundly, and Francia altered the course of the Nuevo Mundo some forty miles and steered her to this stronghold.

Montes—And this fabulous wealth that Francia so often spoke about in his letters?

Talavera—That which the Jews of Spain entrusted to Alvarez to purchase land with in Guiana?

Montes—The same.

Talavera—'Tis clear the Jew must have altered his plans regarding that, and left it in Spain ; still there's a way to get at it.

Montes—Make known the way. I tire of this place, and am constantly importuned by my consort to return again to Spain or some other part of Europe.

Talavera—Had you seized this fortune you might have humored her, and lived forever in the utmost luxury.

Montes—You seem a man of fertile brain, and say this fortune can still be wrung from Alvarez. Now let me hear your plans.

Talavera—Then summon here the Jew and his devoted son. I have seen them cling together so, I know they share but one spiritual life ; no sacrifice would be too great for either one to make to save the other.

Montes—What would you do with them ?

Talavera—Bid the younger find his way again to Spain in my company, holding his father here for ransom, until all of this great wealth is safe within our hands. The youngster will never fail to find it, I warrant you, and I will bear it safely hither.

Montes—You have indeed a brain that works, but my plan is better.

Talavera—Let me hear it.

Montes—We will hold the youth for ransom, and send the father back to Spain.

Talavera—Nay, hear me !

Montes—I know enough of human nature to feel assured, the love we bear our offspring is a thousand times more powerful than that our offsprings give in turn.

Talavera—You misjudge the boy. I tell you ——

Montes—My way is clear. You have found the means, but the manner of their carrying out shall be as I wish.

Talavera—But I tell you——

Montes—I am commander here. Undertake to tell me nothing when once my mind is bent.

Talavera—But my way is surer.

Montes— My way shall be carried out ; and so, for a short time, I leave you. I will have the father sent up from the beach, where he is at work. As for that lily-flavored boy, useless save as ornament. He comes this way together with my consort, who fancies all that's pretty, and seizes on it as her right.

⌊Exits.⌋

Talavera conceals himself behind abutment of the battlements. Enter from castle Estela Alvarez and Angelina Montes.

Angelina—Poor boy ! your sighs find entrance to my longing heart and waft my thoughts to happier days.

Estela—Oh ! surely lady, you who can yet prove gentle 'mid these grim surroundings are capable of being won from them.

Angelina—Had I your spirit, it may have been different with me.

Estela—But, however came you here ?

Angelina—A captive like yourself, I sailed from Spain to join my father in the New World, where he had acquired from the government large tracts of land ; our vessel was attacked as yours, and I was brought to this stronghold a slave awaiting ransom.

Estela—I know you are of gentle birth; and for your breeding, it could grace a palace. How were it possible you could wed a ruffian?

Angelina—Nay, blame me not. Alone and helpless, I assumed at first the cloak of deep reserve ; but he loved me in his own fierce manner and with a warmth that shamed the tropic sun.

Estela—And as the Arctic winds you should have met this love.

Angelina—Alas ! I could not. We are creatures made unconsciously to weld ourselves to habit and fulfill a destiny. Cut off from the world my heart desired still to be of use to some one, in obedience to that strange insistence of our Creator, who gave us these desires with our breath.

Estela—You have the genius to excuse your fault.

Angelina—Ah ! boy, another in my place would chide you for your presumptious tongue, but I love you for it, you remind me ever of the cavaliers of noble birth at home, your aims seem high, your will a marvel, you are the very picture of courage softened by rare beauty.

Estela—I place my faith on High and therefore find this courage, you could have found the means to serve your fellow man and still not linked your life with one of Montes' stamp.

Angelina – Nay ! that I could not Think you, apart, I could have gained so great an influence upon his heart; and do I not use this power to counteract by all the good I can accomplish, his evil acts ; am I not of use to you ?

Estela—Aye, sweet lady, you saved me for your page.

Angelina—When, perhaps, they would have scorched that white face, in the sun's hot rays upon the beach, at labor, such as those soft hands were never made to ———

Estela—And as they have done to my unhappy father.

[Covers her face with her hands.]

Angelina--Be patient, boy, I have sworn to aid you ; and I have seen my chieftain raging in temper like the hurricane, and with a look or touch, I have soothed him into calmness.

Estela—And you will mend my father's sad condition.

Angelina—I will try, my boy; but storms among these men arise as suddenly as the October gales, and therefore, what I tell you now, divulge to no one save your father.

Estela—I will obey you.

Angelina—Should your life be threatened and your limbs unchained, fly with your might along the path that winds up yonder hill. Pause not for breath until you reach the cross that stands upon the summit, cling to that cross, and not a man among this band, be he ever so valorous in battle or bloody in the massacre, will dare lay hands upon you.

Estela.—Impossible ! The cross in my eyes, stands as a symbol of unjust and cruel persecution. It has been carried at the head of crowds, eager to stain the pure sod of my

country, red with my peoples blood, and death I'll welcome
many times, ere I cling to it for life.

Angelina.—But here it will prove your savior, and so
balance the fearful debt it owes you.

Estela.—I thank you, lady ; but know, I set my faith in a
power, higher and greater than a mere symbol of this earth.
No more can I be saved by the wooden cross, than by a tree or
post, for it is invested with no spirit, and can answer no
petition.

Angelina—You are wrong, and speak idly ; a spirit does
pervade it, and has saved already a Christian life and can
save yours, if you will trust it. I have told you;
and if ever in extremity, and will use your knowledge, then you are surely saved. Some slaves approach ; to
see them is to pity them and harrow up the soul. I leave
you here, for among the rest, I see your father.

[Exits.]

Enter Mauricio Alvarez in slaves attire, led by
Ramon Vega and two of the guards.

Vega—Stand here until I call for you.

[Exits with guards.]

Estela—(Rushing to Alvarez) My father !

Alvarez—My beloved child ! how farest thou ?

Estela—Well in health, but tortured in the mind, thinking
of you at your slavish labor in the day, and in your cheer-
less dungeon in the night, and every prayer my brain could
form, and my faltering tongue give utterance, have I offered
up for your relief.

Alvarez—Would we both had died upon the Nuevo
Mundo. ·

Estela—Not so, for hope still lives in me.

Alvarez—But I despair, for escape is impossible.

Estela—Aye ! but even in this place, humanity still sways
the heart of one, and I've been promised aid for you.

Alvarez—By whom ?

Estela—The chieftain's wife.

Alvarez—Has she procured for us this meeting ?

Estela—I know not why you have been brought hither.

Talavera comes from behind the abutment.

Talavera—That I can make known to you.

Alvarez—Dog! I'll not listen to you, you are a traitor, false to your oath, your manhood blasted by as foul a sin as ever merited contempt and death; mock not my helplessness with your presence ; begone !

Talavera—How have I deserved this tirade at your hands.

Alvarez—Think not to deceive these eyes that have pierced the mists of secrets, black as night, and more profound than any you can plan for execution.

Talavera—I do not understand.

Alvarez—You are the one who bade me fly from Cadiz. Spite of the disguise you wore, I know you now.

Talavera—I deny it not, but t'was done to save you.

Alvarez—Had that been so, you would have needed no disguise.

Talavera—Know you not, that he who warns a heretic, forfeits his own life to the Inquisition ?

Alvarez—Pretend not basely to good motives ; that was but the preface to the greater misery you did plot to betray me into.

Talavera—(Hotly.) Nay ! now you say what's false.

Alvarez—Can you thus heap insult upon the victim of your plotting ; nay then, if I die for it, I will throw you headlong · from the battlements.

[Seizes Talavera.]

Talavera—I resist only to save you — (breaks away)—I swear——

Alvarez—No more of oaths ! If earnest in them you would have fulfilled the one so basely uttered on the Nuevo Mundo.

Estela—And partly fulfilled already. Be just and patient, my father ; is it not within his power to make our lot a thousand times more dreadful ?

Alvarez—He has done his very worst.

Estela—Remember, he knows the secret of my sex, which he has not betrayed.

Alvarez - He reserves that for a future torture.

Estela—But forget not that brave act of his which saved me from the lascivious Francia.

Alvarez - Done with some motive that as yet we cannot see.

Talavera—I will make known the motive, that your fears may be at rest - a motive than which no stronger can be named.

Alvarez—And that is——

Talavera—Love !

Alvarez—[Scornfully] Love ! What love can you feel, and for whom?

Talavera--The love that any honest man can feel for a noble woman, and the love I feel is for your daughter.

Alvarez—Serpent ! You love my pure child ! You dare——

Talavera—Ah! What will love not dare ?

Alvarez—Do you hear this monster, child? Curl your proud lip at him that thy disdain may strike him dead. Wretch ! the wrath you have awakened in me, leaves my limbs quivering as though stricken by the palsy. I choke with rage and hatred, or I'd pluck forth the heart that dares presume so high.

Talavera—Hear me !

Alvarez—Child ! child ! pour forth thy eloquence to crush this mischief at its birth.

Estela -[Demurely] My father !

Alvarez—Ha ! Thou speakest with voice subdued and tremulous, when thy tongue should cut and lash as woman's can when honor is assailed ; your eyes, that should dart fire and scorn, are downcast. What can this mean ? Speak !

Estela—Would you have me scorn one to whom I owe more than my life ?

Alvarez--More than thy life ! Has sorrow turned thy brain, or do I dream?

Estela—Love is ever sacred in the eyes of God, and if we cannot meet it with an answering love, oh, let us not mock or curse it.

Alvarez—Thou pleadest for this infidel? Then must I suspect that all my former sorrow was but sport, compared with that which threatens now!

Estela—Fear not, my father. I know our holy law, and if my heart broke in obeying it, I would not falter.

Alvarez—You lift a burden from me, heavier than any I have yet bent under.

Talavera—Fear not danger at my hands. If you but knew me as I am, not what I seem, my presence would be more welcome to you.

Alvarez—Why wear a mask to those powerless to harm you?

Talavera—If I reveal myself, and am overheard, or you betray me, I am lost.

Estela—Confide in us. I'll not believe but that you have a noble heart.

Alvarez—I reserve my judgment till I hear your story.

Talavera—But give me some assurance that what I entrust to you will be divulged to no one.

Alvarez—I will hold it sacred, even though I doubt it.

Talavera—I trust you. I am here a voluntary spy to discover the whereabouts of a lady, a cousin of mine, some five years my senior, and who, leaving Spain to join her father in the New World, ten years ago, is supposed to have been captured by the pirates.

Estela—I know you speak the truth, and Heaven may help me to find her for you. But go on.

Talavera—I had never seen her, but her disappearance was the constant theme of conversation in our family. We appealed to King Philip's Court for assistance in the search in vain. Trouble was then brewing between Spain and England, and all the ships of war were kept at home.

Estela—And Spain's ungrateful court deserted its true subject!

Alavrez—Naught else can be expected from that egotist, King Philip.

Talavera—Seeing this and being fond of venture, I determined to try singly for her rescue. I went to Cadiz, and pretending to be of mean birth, I wandered among the sailors of that port, and learned of the galleon Nuevo Mundo which expected to set sail within a week.

Alvarez—But how came you to warn me of the Inquisition?

Talavera—Disguised as one in want, I met Francia, the mate, at the entrance of your house. We went to the tavern near by, and I wormed myself into his confidence.

Estela—Was it he then who told you to come and warn us?

Talavera—It was. I knew not then his devilish purpose, but came hoping to save you, for I love not the Inquisition, though I am a Catholic.

Estela—But how came you in the Nuevo Mundo?

Talavera—When I left you I rejoined Francia, and he made known to me the fact that he was Montes' agent.

Alvarez—And as Heaven hears you, you shipped on board in order to attempt this rescue?

Talavera—As Heaven is above me, I have told the truth.

Estela—But why did you not warn us or the captain of your knowledge?

Talavera—I feared 'twould foil my purpose.

Estela—And you placed so many innocent souls in jeopardy?

Talavera—Had I betrayed this Francia, alone I could not have found the pirates lair. I had intended that once the harbor sighted, I would warn the captain, and dropping overboard have swum alone to shore.

Estela—That would have been a daring feat.

Talavera—But when I saw the speed with which their boats moved through the water I knew there was no hope, and knowing that I could do more good by passing for a pirate, I let events transpire as they did.

Alvarez—The bitterest curse of the unfortunate light on your head if this is false, but if it be truth ——

Talavera—I will prove the truth of it, with Heaven's help. I have planned already more than one way for our escape.

Alvarez—Escape ? Is such a thing possible ?

Talavera—Anything is possible to one determined as I am. But hush ! here comes the chieftain. Let him not suspect us, or all is lost. Whatever he bids you do 'twere well to follow. Remember, on your discretion much depends.

[Enter Montes.]

Montes (to Alvarez)—So you are here? Briefly, where is that wealth stored that rumor says the Jews of Spain entrusted to you to buy lands in Guiana?

Alvarez—Where none but I can find it

Montes—'Tis well, then, you have left it in Spain. This very night my men shall sail with you to Santa Cruz. You shall have money to pay your passage on a merchant ship, that will touch there two days hence. One year is the most I'll give you to return with all this wealth, and then you and your son shall be free. Come, what say you ?

Alvarez—I am too feeble for the journey. Send my son instead, and I will direct him where to find it.

Montes—You have betrayed the very love that proves the value of my bond. You will return to save your son though all the legions of hell oppose you. This offer is but a plan to save him, and you shall depart alone.

Estela—Nay, mercy ! do not separate us.

Montes—Pshaw ! What know I of mercy ; save your breath. If on the expiration of a year you return not with the ransom, your son shall yield his life as forfeit.

Alvarez—I'll not leave him.

Montes—I will force you hence. My men shall drag you to the vessel, and set sail. Ho, without !

Alvarez—Hold ! Send for your men and I will struggle so, they needs must slay me.

Montes—If you resist, think of the vengeance I will visit on your son.

Alvarez—Are you a man?

Montes—Aye! but one of iron, without a single throb of pity in my heart.

Alvarez—Such men are not born.

Montes—I am one, I tell you, so take leave at once of that toy, or bauble, or gewgaw, whatever you may please to call him, and embark without a moment's loss of time.

Alvarez—'Tis useless. I swear it from my soul, the money has not been left in Spain.

Montes—Then you have it stowed away on board the Nuevo Mundo. Speak! where you have concealed it?

Alvarez—It was hidden by the captain.

Montes—You play with me, I'll have your son lashed and scorched upon his naked back before your eyes, what, ho!

Alvarez—Heaven support me and send me courage!

[Enter Ramon Vega and the two guards.]

Estela—Father, farewell my father I have the means to foil this merciless man. (Takes dagger from her breast). Give me your hasty blessing, ere I die.

Alvarez—My own Estela, light of my eyes, what would you have me do?

Estela—Be steadfast to your oath!

Alvarez—By God's holy law I've sworn to guard my trust. To hundreds of our suffering race, it is the last hope! that's left. I cannot betray it, though we perish.

Estela—Then let us perish. (About to stab herself, Talavera wrests the dagger from her hand). Oh! unkind! unkind!

Alvarez—(To Montes). Stay your ruthless hand, I will yield the fortune.

Montes—Oh! I thought your mind would alter; Talavera, stay and guard the boy; Ramon, follow with the slave.

Montes exits, followed by Alvarez, guarded by Vega and the two guards.

Estela—Alas! his firmness could endure no more. Here comes poor little Duende, the Carib maiden.

[Enter Duende].

Talavera—Not poor, but happy, she lives among the band in better state than any of her people. What has little Duende to care for?

Duende—In my savage state I cared for nothing, but since I have been told of those great countries where you came from, my heart longs to see them.

Talavera—What! would you leave this comfortable fortress? These hills you roam about in perfect freedom, these smiling waters you skim over in your light bark, with such fearless ease?

Duende—What was at first a smouldering ember has become a mighty flame; often have I passed away the day listening to the tales of those strange lands the lady Montes never tires speaking to me of. Is it any wonder for curiosity to grow with learning?

Talavera—But you are happy here?

Duende—No, I am not happy, for I no longer feel content.

Estela—The knowledge she has gained of better things makes her wish for their possession.

Duende—Ere I would live again, as when the Lady Montes found me, a captive in my native village and purchased me for her slave, I'd welcome death.

Estela—So the human heart forever longs for better than it has.

Duende—And are you both from Spain?

Estela—Yes, good Duende.

Duende—Then tell me. (Takes roll of paper from her bosom). Here is what you call a picture, is it not?

[Showing it.]

Talavera—That is right, Duende; this is a picture.

Duende—And these people, they are in the street or square of one of those great cities, the Lady Montes has told me of.

Talavera—You are right, and here are great houses built of heavy stone and rising high as this tower in the air.

Duende—But why is this one figure chained to the post, with lighted fagots all around him ; are they burning him alive?

Talavera—(Sadly). Yes, Duende.

Estela—It is the picture of the dreadful Act of Faith.

[Covers her face with her hands.]

Duende—And so they have this custom also in that gentle country, the Lady Montes so warmly praises ?

Talavera—At the present time they have, good Duende, but it was not always so.

Duende—That's strange, for speaking to me of my race, she told me the people in her land turned faint with horror, when they heard we cooked our captives; and this same one, will all these people, feast upon him when he is burned?

Estela—Peace, good Duende, my flesh creeps to hear you, though you speak in innocence.

Talavera—Nay, these people do it not for the love of inflicting torture, it is all owing to a faulty reasoning, which Heaven in its own time will remedy.

[Estela goes sadly to one side.]

Duende—Ah ! how I should like to visit Spain.

Talavera—You can never hope to do it with your mistress.

Duende—Not visit it with her? Why, she has promised me this very day to take me there when she returns.

Talavera—Which will be never.

Duende—Never ! Why, it is her constant dream.

Talavera—Doomed to disappointment, her husband dare not show his face among these people, for he has disobeyed their laws and treasonably attacked their flag, and if they lay hands upon him they will take his life.

Duende—Can this be true?

Talavera—As sure as you are standing here ; still there's a way, Duende, for you to visit Spain.

Duende-- Oh! name it.

Talavera--It is your custom, when the mood is on you, to wander off among ths hills and live in your little bush huts for days, and you are never missed.

Duende -Ay! for I am restless and cannot live here always, I must see something new, be ever moving.

Talavera— And I have seen how fearlessly you sail your boat upon the harbor.

Duende—Upon the harbor! Nay! I have sailed as far as Santa Cruz and back, all by myself.

Talavera—And know you the way to that Island further West, whose hills faintly break against the horizon.

Duende—I can find it. That is what Lady Montes calls Porto Rico.

Talavera—The same! the very same! Now if you could coast the island in your bark until you reach San Juan, you will see there many Spaniards and ships just like the Nuevo Mundo, which lies moored at the foot of this same cliff. Speak to the people in our tongue and ask for the Governor. That done, give him this letter.

[Takes paper out and writes.]

Duende--I will do it, I do not fear the journey in the least, but how will this——?

Talavera—The Governor will send a vessel here that will take us all to that marvellous country for which you long, the Lady Montes, you and all of us here, but not her husband.

Duende—I care not, because I hate him; when she was not around he has oft' treated me with roughness and even struck me. I love her, but I would as soon see him dead.

Talavera—Embark then, to-night, when all is still.

Duende—I will go at once into the forest and wait till dark; no one shall see the point from which I leave the Island.

[Exits.]

Talavera—One more venture launched.

Enter Evaristo Obregon, carrying a large bundle
of soiled clothing on his back.

Obregon—Maledictions on the work, say I, accursed be the
man who first invented washing.

Talavera—This is the slave to whom I've taken such a
fancy; well, did you eat the bread?

Obregon—Right quickly, and by now 'tis well digested;
but I saved the paper.

Talavera—And you read it? Fear nothing, we are alone,
except the girl, who is a friend.

Obregon—I see no girl, oh! you mean that lad yonder,
he is fair enough to be a girl indeed, but that is nothing.
Rough man as I look, I am counted no better than a woman.

Talavera—In what respect?

Obregon—See you not that they have turned me into a
washerwoman. If I have not this bundle washed by sunset,
no breakfast for me to-morrow.

Talavera—This must, indeed, be maddening to a man of
spirit.

Obregon—Ah! I had lost hope, until I picked that paper
from the bread, or rather I should say coughed it up, for it
was well nigh swallowed, had not Amador delivered me a
slap, right smartly, 'twixt the shoulders, down it would have
gone, and the secret locked within me; still, 'twas a clever
trick, a very clever trick.

Talavera—And when the proper time arrives you will
lend your aid?

Obregon—Aye, if you will promise one thing?

Talavera—And that is?

Obregon—Should we slaves o'ercome the pirates, that
villain, Ramon Vega, shall be my prisoner.

Talavera—'Tis a bargain, but what will you do with him?

Obregon—Fasten one end of an iron chain around his
ankle, like they do prisoners in the chain gang, only instead of a ball at the other end I'll fasten a washtub and

a big bundle of soiled clothing; well, farewell, we must not be seen in conversation.

Talavera—I will find an opportunity to speak in private.

Obregon—Count on my aid in anything; accursed be the man who first invented washing.

> [Exits, hauling out bundle.]

> Enter Montes, Vega, Alvarez and two guards bearing chest, they place chest on stage, down front; enter Angelina Montes. Alvarez staggers to Estela.

Montes—(Dropping on his knees before chest and wrenching open the cover). At last! At last! (To Angelina). Now you shall have your heart's desire, the wealth is mine and we will hence.

Angelina—Forever from these scenes of horror, oh joy! joy! for that.

Estela—My father, all is then taken?

Alvarez-- All that I had saved for thee, Estela. We are penniless Our private wealth I have yielded up.

Estela—But that held in sacred trust?

Alvarez—Remains save within the Nuevo Mundo's hold.

Estela—My noble father.

> Montes takes out two bags from chest, opening one and letting the coin run through his fingers.

Montes—Onzas of gold, every one of them. How many, Jew, does each bag contain?

Alvarez—Each a thousand onzas.

Montes (dropping bag)—And is this the wealth report has likened to a sum five times as great? Cunning wretch! You have concealed it in more than one place.

Alvarez--I swear this is all my wealth. I claim at your hands that freedom promised on its surrender.

Montes—Hope you to purchase freedom with such a trifle? Not you alone shall work until the flesh drop from your.

bones, but your son shall be stripped of his fine feathers, and clad as a slave—wear out his life upon the beach.

Angelina—Nay, Montes, thy compact !

Alvarez—It will naught suffice to further torture me. You are possessed of all I have on earth.

Montes—You cannot deceive me, for I will rend assunder board by board the Nuevo Mundo until nothing but her ribs are left. Thus will I drag the rest of this great fortune to the light ; but for your vile effort at deception you and your son shall work as slaves never worked before. (Pointing to Estela.) Tear from his body those gaudy trappings, and thrust them both without the tower.

Talavera (whispering quickly in Estela's ear as guards advance to obey)—Plead to the lady.

> Estela rushes to Angelina, pursued by the slaves. Angelina stretches out her arms to protect her. Talavera puts out his foot, as if accidentally, tripping up foremost guard.

Estela—Save me ! save me ! I am a woman as thou art.

CURTAIN.

ACT III—SCENE: PLATEAU ON THE MOUNTAIN, AT THE BACK OF WHICH A PRACTICAL ROCKY EMINENCE SURMOUNTED BY A CROSS. SLAVES AT WORK, AMONG THEM MAURICIO ALVAREZ, WHO STANDS ON ONE SIDE LOOKING DOWN THE MOUNTAIN EVARISTO OBREGON AND IGNACIO AMADOR.

Obregon—This fellow gives us hope of freedom.

Amador—Aye, and hope of vengeance also. If I could only fasten these ten fingers in the shaggy locks of that brutal overseer Ramon and tug away until his head parted from his body.

Obregon—Hope it not; his punishment I will inflict. He is to be my prisoner.

Amador—Nay, but you will grant me a tug or two to wipe out old scores.

Obregon—Aye, you may have them, but wrench not his head off

Amador—And wherefore?

Obregon—Because I reserve a punishment, a tthe sight of which all the known torments of Hades will pale with envy.

Amador—Ah! If I only get the chance, how much there is to settle with this villain.

Obregon—No doubt, you have much to complain of, but contrast my state at home with my present condition. True, I was not wealthy, but I did man's work.

Amador—And had, no doubt, a passing good respect for yourself.

Obregon—No sooner was I captured than they chained me to the washtub.

Amador—And bade you wash some forty of their reeking pieces. You have told the story often.

Obregon—Maledictions on them, this was not all. I failed by some five pieces, and in return——

Amador—Received as many lashes. See how well I know.

Obregon—I claim no unclean habits, but I have registered an oath that if ever I live again, with beings that are civilized, I'll wear no clean clothes.

Amador—Not if they can be had without the washing.

Obregon—Aye ! Then, perhaps ; not otherwise. My heart would melt at the sight of a woman at her tub.

Amador—Well, reserve your spite until the time arrives to vent it properly.

[Enter Roberto Talavera.]

Obregon—Here comes our valiant leader.

Talavera—I have prevailed on Ramon to let me play overseer a while. He likes not the neighborhood of the cross, and halts lower down the mountain

Obregon—Have you any further plans to make known to us ?

Talavera—I have not told you that I sent away the little Carib slave for help.

Amador—What ! The child Duende ?

Talavera—Nay, she is no child.

Obregon—Nor yet a woman. But where have you sent her ?

Talavera—To the Governor of Porto Rico.

Amador—Alas ! Alas !

Obregon—'Tis useless. Heaven is against us ; there is no escape.

Amador—We are doomed.

Talavera—Why, what is this ? Was not the move a good one ?

Obregon—Think you this vile band could flourish here were not the Governor of Porto Rico made purposely blind to it ?

Amador—Know you not that Montes pays him well to take no notice of his actions ?

Talavera—Then I have made a move that but doubles our danger.

Obregon—How long ago was this ?

Talavera—'Tis now four days.

Amador—And doubtless, poor little Duende has by force been carried to the mines, to toil her life away.

Talavera—'Tis monstrous.

Obregon—What is to be done ? The Governor may make

report of this to Montes, and then your life will be in danger.

Talavera—I placed not all my hopes upon this plan. I have done good work, whilst others slept.

Amador—In what way?

Talavera—I have hid within the grass, around the foot of yonder cross, a dozen axes that I stole from those, who fell trees on this mountain spur.

Obregon—Ah! more mischief still.

Amador—We both received a dozen lashes for losing those same axes.

Talavera—They were the only weapons I could lay my hands upon.

Obregon—Well, go on.

Amador – Never mind the lashes.

Talavera – I secretly took a boat from off the beach, which now lies moored among the reeds at the foot of this same cliff.

Obregon—And what's your purpose in this?

Talavera—With that we'll risk the passage to Santa Cruz.

Amador—And when shall we attempt it?

Talavera—The time is not far off, for I have gained Ramon, the overseer's, good will. Some night I'll play the jailor in his stead, and release all from their cells. That done, we will meet at this spot.

Amador—But wherefore make not the attempt at once?

Talavera—Have you forgotten the promise made me to succor the lady and her father?

Obregon—Nay, that we have not, and will stand by it, as truly as you stand by us.

[Alvarez comes forward.]

Alvarez—I fear your plans are visionary, and further plotting useless.

Talavera—I shall not cease from trying until you are free, or I am dead.

Obregon—Once rallied round the cross the band will not pursue us.

Talavera—Even if Montes and one or two others of the bravest overcome their superstition enough to make them hazard it.

Alvarez—But cooped upon this summit how shall we live

Talavera—The mountain looking on the sea is broken into ledges, by the aid of ropes, which I have concealed already behind the cross; we can lower ourselves from ledge to ledge until we reach the foot.

Alvarez—And have you warned my girl?

Talavera—I have told your daughter to be prepared upon an instant's notice, to follow me where I shall lead her.

Amador—So be it your care to bring her safely here amongst us.

Obregon—Ramon ascends the pathway!

Talavera—Quick! where is the whip? It grieves me, thus painfully to dissemble, but we must play well our parts, if we would live again with Christians. (Assuming a gruff tone and cracking whip he picks from off the ground). Hey! thou lazy varlet! you have been an hour chopping down that tree and should have had a hundred logs rolled in the valley. Work, I tell you, or I'll crease your body with the lash. (Cracks whip at them, they all caper about, seeming suddenly engaged in work, rolling logs across the stage, etc). Enter Ramon Vega.

Vega—Ha! ha! You make a capital overseer indeed. I warrant me they had no breathing time, whilst I was gone.

Talavera—I made the sweat of labor pour from off their brows. I tell you, you are by far too mild; were I their jailer I would force the music of their groans from them.

Vega—I warrant me you would. (Taking whip.) Hence, curs! Dogs, begone! I need you on yonder crest awhile.

[Snapping whip at them, and driving slaves before him.]

Quick ! for your lives !

> As slaves are driven out, Alvarez reels and falls
> unperceived behind a rock. Exit Talavera
> and Vega following slaves. Enter from op-
> posite side, Estela in woman's clothes and
> Angelina.

Angelina—You come here to cull the flowers, you say.
Is it not because your father works upon the mountain ?

Estela—Aye ! you guess shrewdly. Since I am denied
the happiness of speaking with him, I may at least look
from afar.

Angelina—If I could contrive to have him meet you, I
would, with pleasure do so, and leave you awhile together.

Estela— Would you, indeed. Do you not fear we would
attempt escape ?

Angelina—Nay, you know I saved you from my husband's wrath, by swearing I would ever keep watch, and
prevent your eluding him. You will not get me into
trouble ?

Estela—What ! Repay your kindness with ingratitude ?
Oh, not for all the world.

Angelina—I trust you. The slaves will come this way
again, and then you will have the chance of seeing your
father. I hope it will be soon ; the air is dense and still,
denoting sudden change. I fear one of those storms which
at this season sweep down upon us so unexpectedly. I will
ascend to the Refuge until you call me.

Estela — Stay, Angelina ! sister ! as you have bade me call
you when we were alone together.

Angelina—Well, Estela ?

Estela—Tell me, had you the chance to leave this place,
with all its dismal recollections, would you do so ?

Angelina— Under certain conditions. It is my constant
prayer that such a chance will offer.

Estela—But suppose, that of your family in Spain there
was one brave heart, who, though he never saw you, was

moved by chivalry to risk his life to find and take you from this place?

Angelina—If he found me, I would show by every means I could my lasting gratitude, but who can explain the deep, inscrutable ways of God, who led me to this place, to save perhaps a human soul by winning it to repentance.

Estela—That means, my sister, that you would not leave your husband.

Angelina—You have understood me. Ten years we have lived together for better or for worse, and while I have tried to balance his bad acts by good, and know the hideous color of his deeds, since it has pleased Heaven to cast our lot together, I will not desert him.

Estela—Oh, Angelina!

Angelina—I will leave you now, and when you have seen your father, call me from the foot of the Refuge.

> Angelina and Estela walk to the foot of eminence, which former mounts, disappearing behind the cross.

Estela—Oh, what a fate for such a noble heart!

[She turns to come down stage as Talavera enters front.]

Talavera—Thou here?

Estela—Am I not welcome here, or do I affright thee with my presence?

Talavera—Not so, but when I stand before you, vain, vain regrets o'erwhelm my sinking soul, and tempt me to beseech of Heaven an end of all my misery.

Estela—And if you do, I will beg at once of Heaven to deny it thee. You know I place all hopes of deliverance in you, and if you die, where then, would be my hope?

Talavera—I had the power to save you from this place, and wilfully neglected it.

Estela—Nay, you were moved with feelings of the highest nature, and I blame thee not for my position.

Talavera—Ah, what would I not dare for thee! Danger in any form or shape. Strong as I am, I have not the power to conceal my heart. I am mad! crazed! unhappy! repentant ! and all because I love thee dearer than my live, and see the abyss that yawns between us.

Estela—A gap so wide, that this passion is a misery to both.

Talavera—At least, your heart, like that of mine, is swayed by nature, and the echo of my love is sounded there.

Estela—Ah, brave gentleman ! could I but make thee happy, I would give my life to do it.

Talavera—And yet one little word can do it, which word you will not utter ; and yet, I feel that magnetism, which tells me I have gained your love. Am I not right?

Estela—Aye, I love thee.

Talavera—Sweet Estela !

Estela—But a barrier so great divides us.

Talavera—I will know it, and try to overcome it. Tell me what it is ?

Estela—Turn, as it were, thine eyes towards the country we have left ; see how my unhappy people burrow in dark cellars, like rabbits in their holes ; see how they shun their fellow men, as guilty souls shrink from the light; see how the sod of Spain is tinged with their blood, and how the dreadful Inquisition threatens to grind out the life of man, and woman, and child, if they dare to openly obey the dictates of their conscience. All, all too ! in the name of Him who preached only of charity and good will.

Talavera—But I am not to blame for this.

Estela—Nay, I blame thee not, but I must cling to them in their dark hour, and become a mother amongst my people. We have given to the world a Saviour, and are requited with merciless persecution.

Talavera—Can I not join, and risk with thee the fury of thy persecutors ?

Estela—Thine own race are possessed of women unrivalled for their goodness, who have in them the power to weld by infinite charm the character and the fortune of man Seek one from amongst them to walk through life with thee.

Talavera—Think you the heart can be controlled thus lightly, to bid it fasten its affections at it owner's will? Nay, the fire of love leaps swiftly, and with overwhelming force, taking possession ere you can guard against its sweet assault. To wrest thine image from my heart, would leave its soil so barren, no seeds of love could flourish there again.

Estela—Nay, love is never wasted. Be it futile, the power remains to soften and refine the heart that suffers. I love thee with equal warmth, and must suffer as you do, and still I force myself, in obedience to a higher duty, to tell thee, that night and morn I'll beseech God's mercy on your welfare, but I can never wed thee.

> Mauricio Alvarez, who during the conversation has recovered and been a listener to it, now comes forward with a feeble step.

Alvarez—Estela, my daughter!

Estela—Father, my beloved father!

Talavera—How came you here, sir?

Alvarez—I fell exhausted, and Ramon drove past the other slaves without perceiving me. (To Estela.). I saw thee coming up the mountain with that noble friend, the Lady Montes. Ah! how my greedy eyes devoured thy fair form, my daughter; how my trembling arms longed to enfold thee in this embrace.

Estela—And you have overheard my frank confession?

Alvarez—I have, and also beheld your strength of purpose, and adherence to our law. I blame you not, Roberto, for loving her. Who could see her pure face, and know her woman's heart, and not desire to link their lives with hers?

Talavera—Ah! who, indeed? And those who once loving her, and are refused that happy privilege, are consigned for ever to the shades of melancholy.

Alvarez—Say not that, for I do grieve for you, as though you were a son, and to see you happy is to be so myself. (To Estela.) Perhaps, child, your mind may alter as regards Roberto?

Talavera—Urge not her noble .spirit from its .bent. I am at least a man and will not plead for that which is denied me, and so to wrest the subject from my mind let me tell you that your treasure is safe.

Alvarez—Safe! the treasure safe!

Talavera--Stealing on board the Nuevo Mundo in the dead of night, I sawed from its hiding place the chest, con-taining the ten bags of gold, that cause you so much anx-ious care.

Alvarez--And now, where are they now?

Talavera—Buried at the foot of yonder cross.

Alvarez--Brave friend, I owe you more than life. Estela, child, he has saved our race, how shall we reward him?

Talavera--The reward I look for is to see you and your daughter safe again; what becomes of me, I care not; but conceal this weapon on your person; this very night shall we attempt escape, and it may be of service to you. (Draws dagger from his belt, and gives it to Mauricio. During con-versation, Stage becomes darker gradually, and distant thunder is heard, growing nearer every moment).

Alvarez—(Concealing weapon in his breast.) God grant our plans may thrive, but I fear, indeed, my strength is going.

Estela-- Have courage yet awhile, my father.

Alvarez—My many trials, fast hurry me to my un-timely end.

Estela—Live for my sake, and for the fulfillment of thy trust.

Talavera—Once away from this vile hole, your courage will revive.

Estela—Oh, Heaven! If any life is needed as a sacri-fice for our escape, take mine, I implore thee.

Alvarez—Nay, who would not rather see the blossom ripen to a flower, to yield the earth fresh blossoms.

Estela—Life, to me, without your presence would be valueless.

Alvarez—I can die at peace, leaving thy dear self to fill

whatever gap 1 make ; this faintness comes on me again. Roberto support me!

> Reels. Talavera supports him. He sinks in a sitting posture on a rock.

Talavera—Courage ! Courage !

Alvarez—Oh ! how can I ever tell thee, my beloved child, what most I would desire, being so contrary to what I always bade thee ?

Estela—My father, your desires are laws to me.

Alvarez—And, therefore, the duty that I owe to thee, is a thousand times more binding; perhaps I cannot stay to guide thy footsteps on this fleeting earth, but I would leave thee happy.

Estela—What would you have me do?

Alvarez—We stand upon the threshold of a new world. Shall we bring to it the prejudices that have made the old a place of such torment ?

Estela—I do not understand you, father.

Alvarez—That noble symbol, too oft, alas ! the subject of a sneer from our race, rears its proud form as guardian to my trust.

Estela—Of what do you speak?

Alvarez—The holy cross, for here its purposes are holy, the one spot in all this isle where the persecuted can find a refuge.

Talavera—Standing alike, for those of any creed.

Alvarez- -And then, this noble follower of the cross, my brave Roberto, dear child of nature, with a heart of love for all his fellow men, does he not risk his life, for those of our race, who wait at home, with trembling eagerness, for a summons to this land of promise ?

Estela—Aye ! he is noble in thought and deed.

Alvarez—And does he not love thee. Speak again, Roberto. Do you not love Estela?

Talavera—With all the power of my soul.

Alvarez—And while thou livest, she shall never want for a protector ?

Talavera—If Heaven will only let me ever dwell by her side, she shall not.

Alvarez--Then, Estela, turn not from him, on account of faith, but join your life with his, and strengthen thus the kin of all humanity.

Estela—My father! Can you weaken my already faltering heart, by such sweet advice.

Alvarez—Advice, which is the fruit of earnest thought, Estela!

Estela—But our suffering people, how can I reconcile my heart to this desertion?

Alvarez—Has not Roberto saved for them, much more than you could give, by simply joining life with one, your heart belonging to another?

Estela—Aye! in saving you, he has.

Alvarez—The treasure! Have you forgotten? He has at his most serious peril, taken from the galleon, and brought it here.

Estela—Brave Roberto!

Alvarez--One word from him, and that rock of hope for our race would have been shattered into pieces: but the sun is getting low, and clouds are gathering. No more at present. Roberto, see her safely to the castle.

Talavera—Leave her to my care. 'Twere well you joined the others 'ere you are missed.

Alvarez—We must be careful how we meet, for since that day my wealth was wrung from me, and Estela made known her sex, I have been constantly dogged by the cruel Montes. Farewell.

Talavera--Remember, to-night we make the attempt.

Alvarez--I leave all to you. Farewell, Estela. Think on what I have said to thee.

Estela--I will, my father.

       Alvarez about to go, when Montes steps suddenly from behind the rocks into his path.

Montes—Stay, Jew.

Talavera—Montes!

Montes—Aye! Montes, traitor. I can play the spy as well as leader.

Estela—God be merciful !

Montes—I have overheard your entire conversation ; so you had hopes of deceiving me, eh? The wealth already yielded up was not all. I thought it smaller than report had made it ; and, therefore, kept you still a captive awaiting such a chance.

Alvarez—Lost ! all lost !

Montes—Ha ! Ha ! it lies buried near the cross, eh ! Good !

Talavera—Despicable hound! We are alone ; draw and defend yourself.

[Draws sword.]

Montes--Not yet.

[Blows whistle. Guards armed with spears, rush in.]

Alvarez—All lost ! Close to my side, Estela.

Montes (to Talavera)—I am not alone, and for your treachery, upon the barbican in chains I'll hang you, and let the vultures glut their appetite upon your flesh.

Enter Ramon Vega, driving slaves before him.

Talavera—The slaves returning ! Then there's hope.

Montes (to Alvarez)—As for your lily-faced daughter, whom my weak-hearted consort prevailed on me to spare—ha ! ha !—I'll give her to my faithful overseer Ramon for wife. Ramon, seize on the woman ; she is yours.

[Lightning becomes more vivid.]

Alvarez—Roberto, guard her. (Yields Estela quickly to Talavera, and takes a step or two towards Montes, feeling for dagger in his sack.) Ah, Heaven sends succor ! Behold a fleet of vessels flying the English flag, makes for the harbor. We are saved !

[Points suddenly to harbor.]

Montes—Maledictions ! Where ?

[Turns his head to look. Alvarez draws dagger quickly, and stabs him. He falls on his knees.]

Montes—Undone ! Vengeance has overtaken me at last, but you shall perish as I do. On men ! Fear not the Refuge—idle tales—a dying man refutes them—dig—dig--for the treasure. Oh, I am lost ! Ramon, avenge me. Seize the woman ! Guards, hurl them from the cliff !

> Writhes upon the ground. Guards, headed by Vega, advance to seize Talavera and Alvarez.

Talavera—Fly ! Fly to the cross for aid.

> Estela hesitates a second, looking towards her father, who points up the ascent. They rush up to the cross, followed by the slaves, who pick axes from the ground, and raise them in defence.

Montes (clinging to rocks, and drawing himself up)—They think we fear the Refuge. Prove that ye are men but once again. Support me, and I'll lead.

> Ramon and a guard support him. They level their spears, and advance. The storm rages. Angelina Montes, heavily veiled in white, steps from behind the cross, and stretches out her arms. The lightning flashes on her.

Vega—Fly ! Fly, men ! It is the spirit of the cross.

> Guards exit precipitately. Ramon Vega pauses to lay the fainting form of Montes on the ground, and is swooped down upon by Amador and Obregon, who haul him down front Angelina kneels by her husband, and raises his head tenderly. The storm passes away gradually.

Obregon (striking Ramon Vega)--That is for the blow you gave me yesterday.

Amador—I have sworn to pluck out your hair. Take that ! (Tugs at his hair.)

Vega--Mercy ! Spare me !

Obregon—Aye ! We'll spare you, to wash the clothes of every sailor in yon fleet, and perform what other menial task you have made me slave at.

[They exit, hauling Vega with them.]

Talavera—Free ! Free ! Men from the fleet are entering the castle. The pirates fly to the mountains.

Alvarez—Delivered by a force of the Reformed Church. We need not fear my daughter to make ourselves known.

Estela—See ! Our noble friend weeps over the body of her husband.

Alvarez—Let us not forget her goodness in the dark hour of her adversity.

Estela—I will go and comfort her.

Alvarez—Do so, while I rest myself here. I feel exhausted. (Sits on rock.)

[Estela comes down to Angelina.]

Estela—So you are the spirit of the cross? To you we owe our lives. Would then, that none of mine had visited sorrow on you

Angelina—I had hoped in time to wean him from this place, and live in honor once again at home, but Heaven's ways are just. 'Tis better that he die thus, than perish on the gibbet.

Estela—Why weep you so bitterly, then?

Angelina—Alas ! In a vale amongst the mountains, screened from view, is our child's grave. In that we had a mutual sorrow, and a tie that knit our lives together.

Duende enters hurriedly. Talavera runs to her. placing his finger on his lips to caution silence. They go aside.

Duende—I was picked up by an English ship, ere I had been six hours at sea.

Talavera--And why did you not come sooner ?

Duende—They read my letter, but could not understand the language, but as it was Spanish, they kept me prisoner.

Talavera—True ! England is at war with Spain, and, no doubt, Porto Rico is to be attacked.

Duende—We sailed about for three days, until joined by other ships. A Spanish prisoner on one of them read the letter, and told its meaning, and they sailed towards this Island. The castle is taken !

Talavera—Aye, and your cruel master dead ; but never let your mistress know what part you have taken in this bloody work, or she will hate you.

Duende—Never ! But shall we not have the chance now to live in Spain ?

Angelina (crying out)—Oh ! let not his body suffer base indignity ; his crimes are atoned by death. I would bury him in secret, and pray over his grave. If captured by the enemy, this will be denied me.

Estela—What can be done ?

Angelina (to Estela)—To you I look for aid. Remember what you owe to me.

Estela—Roberto, aid her in her wish, ere the English seize his body.

Talavera—I cannot. 'Twere a mockery to grant him holy burial.

Estela—I implore you !

Talavera—Nay, ask it not. If this were done, there is no virtue in the peace the grave grants an honest man.

Estela—Roberto, through the grief-stricken heart that bemoans his death courses the same blood as your own.

Talavera—What mean you by that, Estela ?

Estela—That stricken woman, is your cousin !

Talavera—God ! I have suspected it.

Estela—For whom you risked your life !

Talavera—Most undeservedly ; had she retained her honor, or lost it opposing, with her might, the savage ruffian, I could have felt for her ; but to mix her blood with such———

Estela—Peace, Roberto ! Had we not met her here, what would have been my fate ?

Talavera—Had she not been here, no more would we.

Estela—Roberto, I have looked upon you as a hero; stain not your noble manhood with this cruelty.

Talavera—This is not cruelty, but justice. Think of the torture I have suffered, when I have seen the thickening dangers, gathering around you, and I, suffering with you in spirit, and standing by so helpless.

Estela—If, for the love of me, you feel this vengeance, then, for that love, I ask you to forego it.

Talavera—I yield, Estela, for your sweet sake. I'll aid her, but she must know nothing of the fact, that I am her cousin.

Estela—Why not, Roberto !

Talavera—Let it be as secret as the grave. She can then return to Spain, and live without the fear of any one who knows her history.

Estela—Well thought of, on your part, Roberto !

Talavera—(To the slaves). Men, I have given you freedom ; do now, what I ask of you.

Slave—Speak ! We will do anything you ask.

Talavera—Bear the body to the summit, and lower it gently in the boat ; use the sling I had prepared for the lady. Duende, come here !

Duende—What can I do ?

Talavera—But one thing more is required of you.

Duende—And that is——?

Talavera—Sail with your mistress and her husband's body to Santa Cruz, through the narrow channel to the West, where the English cannot see you. In a few days you will have a ship there, bound for Spain.

Duende—Anything for the Lady Montes. .

Slaves bear Montes body up the ascent, followed
by Angelina, Estela, Duende and Talavera.

Angelina—Farewell, Estela ! Pray for your unhappy sister, who shall ever think of you.

Estela—Farewell forever, Angelina, and may Heaven shower on you all its richest blessings.

> They embrace. Slaves, Angelina and Duende disappear behind the cross. Talavera and Estela join hands, and come slowly towards Mauricio Alvarez.

Estela—Ah! I hope this is the last sad parting for this day.

Talavera—It all depends on you, Estela. Shall I return to Spain, or cast my fortune with you in Guiana?

Estela—If my lips could only frame the words, my heart urges them to frame!

Talavera—Remember what thy father said, let not the prejudice of the Old infect us in the New World. Come, now, your answer.

Estela—Then let my father answer.

Talavera—(Rising with sudden vigor). As your hands are joined, so too, join your hearts and lives. The lesson of this happy hour is the potency of love, above all things human in this fleeting life. Implanted in our hearts by the Creator, to stem in time, the torrent of that prejudice, from which every faith in turn has suffered, and prove the human race kinsmen, with a common destiny.

> Talavera and Estela embrace. Alvarez raises his arms, outstretched above them.

[Curtain.]

Copyright, 1888.

By I. WOLFF.